CALUM'S NEW BOOTS

For Mum, the greatest teacher I ever had – D.S.

For Enki, my pride and joy – and my inspiration
for drawing Calum! – A.A.M.

Young Kelpies is an imprint of Floris Books
First published in 2016 by Floris Books

Text © 2016 Danny Scott. Illustrations © 2016 Floris Books
Danny Scott and Alice A. Morentorn have asserted their rights
under the Copyright, Designs and Patent Act 1988 to
be identified as the Author and Illustrator of this work

The publisher acknowledges subsidy from
Creative Scotland towards the publication
of this volume

MIX
Paper from
responsible sources
FSC® C007785
FSC
www.fsc.org

This book is also
available as an eBook

British Library CIP data available
ISBN 978-178250-264-7
Printed in Great Britain
by Bell & Bain Ltd

CALUM'S NEW BOOTS

written by **Danny Scott**

illustrated by **Alice A. Morentorn**

ERIKA
BROWN

CALUM
FERGUSON

LEO
NKWANU

LEWIS BUDGE

MR MCKLOP

BRANDON CRAMOND

RAVI GUPTA

JORDAN MCPRIDE

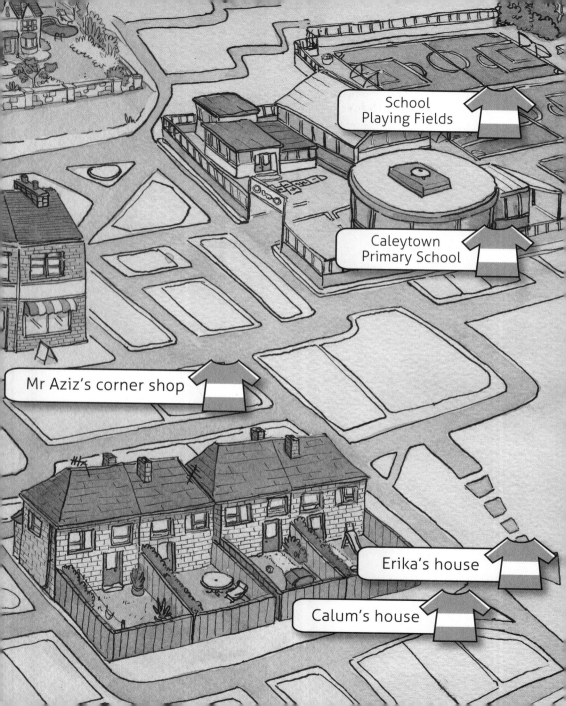

School
Playing Fields

Caleytown
Primary School

Mr Aziz's corner shop

Erika's house

Calum's house

Goal for Scotland

"*Come on referee!*" Calum and his friend Mr Aziz shouted at the screen.

They were standing in Mr Aziz's shop watching Scotland play on the shopkeeper's big flat-screen television. Leighton, Calum's dog, showed his disgust at the decision by barking. They *all* knew that barking wouldn't do much good, but the pressure was on. Scotland needed a win to qualify for next summer's tournament.

Scotland's coach is making a gamble – he's bringing on the uncapped striker from King's Park Athletic, James Cauldfield, as a replacement.

Calum's frustration turned to joy as his favourite player stood, puffing his cheeks out, ready to come on.

James Cauldfield was a local hero. He was born in Caleytown, had gone to Calum's school and was now the top goalscorer at King's Park Athletic – the club everyone in Caleytown supported.

"Hey 'Caleytown's gifted number nine', did I miss much?" said Leo as he burst through the shop door with a soggy piece of paper in his hand. His afro was shining from the light drizzle outside.

"James Cauldfield is coming on for his Scotland debut!" said Calum.

"Sweet!" said Leo.

"Caleytown's gifted number nine?" Mr Aziz asked.

Leo waved the piece of paper he was holding in the air. "It's from our Muckleton match report. A blogger on Scotland Stars F.C. is a *big* Calum Ferguson fan!"

On the TV, James Cauldfield was now battling in the rain, trying to break the deadlock for Scotland. Leo started to read out the match report. All the players at school were obsessed with the Scotland Stars F.C. website. Leo grimaced when he got to the bit about their teammate Jordan.

"...*Jordan McPride gave Caleytown hope in the dying seconds of the first half with a deflected goal...*"

"A total fluke," said Calum.

"*Well* jammy," agreed Leo, before carrying on with the report. "...*Hope soon turned to excitement when Leo Nkwanu danced down the sideline to wow the crowds with some stellar* footwork and set Calum Ferguson up for the equaliser."

Calum and Leo grinned at each other and high-fived.

Leo continued, "...*No one could have guessed that Caleytown's gifted number nine would b—*"

"Penalty!" shouted Mr Aziz, pointing at the screen above them.

The boys turned to look. With the score at 0–0, and the clock deep into injury time, James Cauldfield was face-down on the ground with the soles of his yellow boots in the air. An opposition defender held his hands up – he looked like he feared the worst.

The referee jogged into the box and pointed to the penalty spot.

Mr Aziz, Leo and Calum all turned to each other with crazy grins on their faces. This was it! A golden chance for Scotland to sneak a win.

James Cauldfield's got the ball in his hands. He's going to take this vital penalty on his Scotland debut. What guts he has, this young kid from... erm... Caleytown.

Leo turned to Calum, "He just said 'Caleytown'!"

"I know!"

Mr Aziz shushed the boys and a hush fell

over the shop. All you could hear was the low buzz of the fridges.

...James Cauldfield is placing the ball for what will surely be the last kick of the game...

...He's waiting for the Swiss referee to blow his whistle.

PEEP!

James Cauldfieeeeeeeld SCORES! Scotland win!

Scotland WIN!

"YAAAAAASSSSS!" Leo and Calum jumped up and down and hugged. Mr Aziz shook both his fists above his head so hard that his moustache jiggled. Leighton barked.

"Excuse me, are you still open?" An older woman stood at the shop door with a puzzled look on her face.

Mr Aziz fixed his hair and clothes. "Of course we are, madam. My apologies."

Toe Poke

The next morning, for once, Calum wasn't running late for school.

Instead, he was walking through the streets of identical houses in his estate, talking football with his neighbour Erika.

Erika had recently moved to Scotland from the USA. Her 'mom' was a 'soccer-crazy' American and had started coaching the P6 girls' football team the moment she arrived in Caleytown.

Erika and Calum spotted Leo waiting for them outside Mr Aziz's shop.

Leo's hair still had a dent in it from his pillow. He looked groggy. "Sleep well, Leo?" Erika laughed.

"Huh?" Leo rubbed sleep from his eyes. "I couldn't sleep after Cauldfield's penalty." He and Calum bumped fists.

"Oh, Scotland has a team?" Erika teased.

"I've seen the US teams at the men's *and* women's World Cup Finals but I've never seen Scotland play."

Calum and Leo rolled their eyes.

"Speaking of tournaments, my mom says there's some big news for both school teams today. She wouldn't say what."

Hearing that, Calum and Leo picked up the pace, rushing to school to find out the big news.

There was going to be a meeting at lunch time, but rumours were already spreading fast. During their kickabout at break, Jordan was whispering to Caleytown's P6 goalkeeper Ravi and red-haired midfielder Lewis. He had popped the collar up on his polo shirt.

A few other players hung about waiting for a game to start.

"If Mr McKlop's got another match planned, I'd better be playing up front this time," Jordan said in Calum's direction.

Calum was busy putting on the old, battered boots Mr Aziz had given him.

Upset at getting no response, Jordan tried again. "Haven't you returned your boots to the museum yet?" He laughed at his own joke.

"I'll do it next week," Calum said, to take the wind out of Jordan's sails. "After my dad buys me a brand new pair from Total Soccer this Saturday."

The corner of Jordan's collar flopped down.

Saturday can't come soon enough. Calum grimaced as the old boots dug into his heels and scratched the tops of his feet. The left one was taped up because it had split open during the last big match.

The players formed teams of two for a game of doubles. Leo went with Calum, and Jordan paired up with Lewis. Caleytown's blond central defender Janek formed a team with the wiry right wingback Ryan.

In goals, Ravi checked his precious quiff one last time before sliding on his gloves, picking up the ball and kicking it straight to Jordan.

Jordan only just controlled the ball before shouting from outside the box. "Let me show Museum Boots how it's done."

Although he was a pretty good defender, Jordan wasn't so hot with the ball at his feet.

"Wait for it," Leo said under his breath to Calum when Jordan set off on a solo dribble. Lewis tried to stay open for a pass but even he knew a pass wasn't going to come his way.

Sure enough, Jordan barely made it past Ryan before he lost control of the ball. Calum leapt on it and fired a pass to Leo. Calum tried to ignore the old boots nipping at his heels with every step as he ran into space.

Leo spotted the run and threaded a through pass between the other pairs.

"This'll be fun," Calum heard Jordan scoff as Ravi ran out to narrow the angle, the stylish keeper's big quiff of hair blocking out even more of the goal.

With no time to shoot, Calum took the ball past Ravi, who wasn't up for diving on the damp Astroturf.

"I'll show you, McPride," Calum said through gritted teeth. He planted his right foot and was about to smash the ball into the empty net when...

CreCHHHHHHH

Calum's right foot popped out through a new hole in the front of his boot. Off balance, Calum flapped at the ball with his left foot but only managed to tap it wide of the open goal.

"Ah ha ha ha ha!" Jordan howled, holding his sides just to make sure everyone knew exactly how much he was laughing. The others joined in, even the defender Janek, who was normally quite quiet.

"Yep, Saturday can't come soon enough," Calum muttered to himself.

Edinburgh-bound

Mr McKlop, Calum's teacher and the coach of the football team, burst into the gym hall for the P6 teams' lunchtime meeting. Coach Brown, Erika's mum, strode in behind him.

"Good afternoon, ladies and gentlemen!" Mr McKlop said. "We've got some pretty exciting news for you."

Coach Brown stepped forward, a clipboard in her hand. With her reddish hair and sporty build, she looked like a grown-up version of

Erika. "Listen up!" she shouted. Everyone did.
"Now, how many of you guys have been to
Edinburgh?"

Calum didn't put his hand up. He'd never visited Scotland's capital city. He'd spent his whole life in the Highlands until his family had moved to Caleytown in the summer. He'd seen pictures though.

"About half of you? Well, I've got some good news for y'all," she continued. "Coach McKlop and I have accepted an invitation from a school there called Castle Rock Primary to take part in their annual tournament. It's in a couple weeks' time."

Noisy chatter filled the hall.

"So we need two things from y'all," Coach Brown continued. "One: that you get your folks' permission to come. And two: that y'all promise to show them city folks how we play soccer here in Caleytown!"

Both teams let out a big cheer, apart from Erika, who just looked a bit embarrassed by her competitive mum.

"One more thing," Mr McKlop said, frowning at all the noise. "The boys' team's training session will be in the computer room today, not on the pitch."

"What... why?" Jordan asked.

"You'll see," was all Mr McKlop said before he disappeared out the door.

Later, at 'training', the boys' team sat down, two to a computer, waiting for instructions. Outside they could see the girls' team playing on the pitches in the sunshine.

"I'm amazing on computers," Jordan boasted. "I once got an email from an MI5 agent asking if I'd be interested in doing some work for them – no joke!"

"Then why are you holding the mouse the wrong way round?" Leo asked.

Jordan's cheeks flushed. "I'm used to working on tablets, alright? Using a

mouse is *so* last century."

"Right, squad," Mr McKlop clapped his hands together, "you must be wondering why we're all in here."

The whole team looked outside longingly.

"All the clubs, like King's Park Athletic, employ people to research each team they're going to play."

Calum and Leo nodded along. Jordan quietly turned his mouse the right way round.

"So that's what we're going to do today," Mr McKlop continued as he strode around the computer desks. "You'll be playing these three teams in Edinburgh." He scrawled on the whiteboard in his messy writing:

Castle Rock — Edinburgh

Minch — Glasgow

Burvie — Scottish Borders

"In your pairs, I want you to find out as much as you can about each team," said Mr McKlop. He blew a short burst on his whistle as if they were kicking off a match.

Each pair started furiously clicking and typing.

Leo and Calum knew exactly where they'd search first. Whenever they weren't on the pitch, they were on the Scotland Stars F.C. site.

"Click on the 'Edinburgh and Lothians' page," Calum said, his eyes darting about the screen like a wasp trapped behind a window.

HOME NEWS LEAGUES PLAYERS CALENDAR

ANNUAL CASTLE ROCK PRIMARY TOURNAMENT

Castle Rock Primary School is hosting its annual invitational tournament in Holyrood Park this month, featuring boys' and girls' teams from Minch, Burvie and Caleytown.

Calum and Leo found some links to match reports about Minch and Burvie. They were obviously good teams. Minch had a tall centre-back who seemed to score a lot of goals – for a defender. And judging by their team photograph, Burvie were a strong bunch of lads.

"Hey guys, come and look at this," shouted Ravi. His quiff was quivering.

The Cramond Challenge

The boys gathered round Ravi's computer. His hands flew about the keys like he was playing the piano. A video popped up on his screen.

"Can I click play, sir?" he asked.

Mr McKlop nodded. "Good work, Ravi."

A presenter their age appeared on the screen:

> Here we are at Castle Rock's training session to catch up with Brandon Cramond – Castle Rock's P6 captain who also plays for Hibernian's highly rated under-10 team.

The video cut to footage of Brandon Cramond nutmegging two players before curling a perfect shot into the top corner.

Nerves began to crackle and pop in Calum's stomach.

The presenter reappeared with a microphone, next to Brandon Cramond himself.

So, Brandon, how do you rate your chances in Castle Rock's upcoming tournament?

Thanks Reiss. Well, I've been on great form this year so far. If the rest of my team do as I say, I'm confident we can smash Burvie, Minch and... who cares about the other team. I've never even heard of them.

A smile crept across his face. He had black hair and dark eyes. Smiling didn't come naturally to him: it seemed like something he'd practised in front of the mirror.

The interviewer glanced at the next question on his sheet, gulped, then looked up at the team captain.

So, Brandon, in Castle Rock's last game, some people accused you of injuring Stockfield's star striker on purpose?

Calum watched as Brandon turned to the interviewer and stared at him as though he'd just sneezed on his lunch. Brandon's eyes had become as black as coals. It felt like the temperature dropped in the computer room.

I'd say, *Reiss*, that, if those people knew what was good for them, they'd keep their opinions to themselves.

The interviewer winced, turned back to the camera and tried to smile.

Brandon Cramond, everybody. Come watch him in action against Minch, Burvie and... erm... Caleytown, a week on Saturday at Holyrood Park. This is Reiss Robertson reporting for Scotland Stars F.C.

The computer room was silent. All the team could hear was distant shouting from the girls' training session outside.

"See..." said Mr McKlop finally, after a long pause, "it's always a good idea to know who you'll be up against."

Calum's New Boots

Calum got up so early on Saturday that even Leighton groaned and hid his eyes under his paws.

Calum wasn't going back to sleep though. Not on the day he was getting new boots. Castle Rock's tournament in Edinburgh would be played on grass, but Scotland Stars had advised players to wear Astroturf boots because the ground was still really hard from summer's hot weather.

After two long hours of watching his dad eat breakfast, check the news and do other boring stuff, Calum was finally sitting next to him on a bus headed to Caleyfield shopping centre.

"Do you know which boots you want?" Calum's dad asked, putting his arm round his son's shoulders.

Calum thought about it for a second. "I'd like a yellow pair to match our strip."

"Yellow?!" his dad asked, as if he didn't believe you could get yellow boots.

"Uh-huh, yellow. James Cauldfield wears yellow boots."

His dad smiled. "Fair enough."

When they walked into Total Soccer, Calum's eyes grew as big as two footballs. One side of the shop was completely filled with football boots. The other side was packed with strips from all the biggest clubs in the world.

Down the middle of the shop was everything else a football player could possibly need. You could buy all types of shin pads, goalkeeper

gloves, footballs, thermal vests, socks, and water bottles from a huge water-bottle tower.

So this is where Jordan gets all his fancy gear, thought Calum. All Calum wanted, though, was a new pair of astros.

At first, there seemed to be far too many to choose from. Calum's head was spinning from looking at a rainbow of blue boots, pink boots, red boots and green boots. There were even pairs of boots with a different colour for each foot.

"Wow," Calum's dad said. "Do they do boots in plain old black any more?"

"Just plimsolls, Dad," Calum said. His dad, who'd only just discovered that no one wore plimsolls any more, shoved him gently away. By the time Calum recovered his balance, something had caught his eye. In the bottom corner of the display, half-hidden by the cardboard cut-out of a footballer, sat a bright yellow astro boot. It was pointing in the other direction from all the other boots on display.

"This is it," Calum said, holding it up to his dad as if he'd found buried treasure.

Calum's dad quickly checked the price tag. "Alright, I'll get someone over."

He waved at a shop assistant who was hanging about near the water bottles.

His fringe was swept down over his face so he kept having to blow it out of his eyes with a 'pfft'.

When he got closer, Calum saw that his name badge said 'Malcolm'.

"Where did you find *these*, wee man, pfft?" asked Malcolm. After measuring Calum's feet he glanced back at the display shoe. "Not sure if we'll have 'em in your size – I'll check though, pfft."

It took Malcolm forever to come back. Calum tried to distract himself by looking at shin pads but all he could think about were those yellow boots.

"You're in luck!" Malcolm said when he finally returned. "There was only one pair left, and it was in your size! Give them a go, pfft."

Calum slid them on. It was like sliding a pair of gloves onto his feet.

"How do they feel, Cal?" his dad asked.

"They're perfect!" Calum said to his feet.

"Are you *absolutely* sure now?" his dad asked cautiously. "I'm not coming all the way back here to change them."

"Pfft," Macolm blew the hair out of his eyes and looked around the empty shop. "Listen wee man... pfft, we don't normally do this but would you like to try them out with a football to make sure?" The shop assistant winked under his fringe.

He picked up a ball and tossed it to Calum.

In his new boots, Calum didn't even bother to catch it first. He brought the ball under his spell straight away and did a few keepy-uppies.

"Hey, you're pretty good wee man, here, pfft, gimme a shot before my manager gets back." Malcolm grinned like they were raiding the biscuit tin together.

Calum passed the ball through the air to the shop assistant.

Malcolm had a good touch but his balance wasn't great. Plus, his hair kept falling into his eyes.

"*Careful...*" Calum's dad said with his arms outstretched as Malcolm started to lose control.

It was too late.

Malcolm hoofed the ball towards the tower of water bottles in the middle of the shop... and...

CRASH!

The tower collapsed like a house of cards.

The shop assistant's face turned white as his boss appeared from the storeroom, roaring "MALCOLM!"

Calum's dad quickly took the boots to the till and paid. Calum could tell that he was trying his hardest not to burst out laughing.

6

That's Why They Call Them Castle Rock

The week leading up to the tournament went by at a snail's pace.

Jordan spent every break boasting about how many times he'd visited Edinburgh. *Apparently*, his dad was arranging for scouts from Hearts and Hibs to come and watch him play. Only his crew of Lewis, Ravi and Ryan pretended to believe him.

In the hallway of his house, Calum's mum was busy stuffing Mr Aziz's boots into his bag.

"Mum, why do I need to take those scaffy old boots too?" Calum whined. "They're ripped anyway."

"Just in case you get blisters in your fancy new ones," she replied, zipping up his bag. "I've taped the right boot up now too. They're as good as new."

"I doubt it. And anyway, I've been wearing my new astros all week," Calum protested. In fact, he couldn't stop scoring in them. He felt like a new player.

"Better safe than sorry, Cal," his dad said. "Mum knows best, ok?"

Calum sighed.

"Have a good time Calum," his mum said, looking like she might cry. "Edinburgh's a great place. It's where I met your dad. Remember to look out for the castle."

"Can I go now?" Calum sighed. "You're making me late... *again.*"

"Punctual as ever, Mr Ferguson," Mr McKlop said as Calum ran towards the bus.

"Sorry Mr McKlop," Calum said, "it was my mum's fault."

"Now, now, Calum." Mr McKlop smiled. "Don't be a tell-tale."

It smelt like a damp attic on board the bus and the seats were a sickly orange-and-brown pattern.

"We're lucky," Leo said, moving his bag off the seat he'd been saving for Calum. "Manchester United weren't using their tour bus this weekend so they said we could borrow it."

Calum laughed.

"By the way," Leo yawned, "I'll probably fall asleep. I always fall asleep on buses."

Leo wasn't joking. The bus had hardly got to the end of the street before the rumble of its engine had him snoring into the window.

Up the back, Jordan was making everyone listen to a playlist he'd made especially for the trip. He had persuaded the driver to put it on through the bus's speakers, and was now trying to show off by rapping along to one of the tunes.

"Jordan, please stop," said Erika's friend Sally. "You're making me travel sick!"

With no one to speak to, Calum couldn't keep his mind off Brandon Cramond, Castle Rock's scary midfielder. What if the rest of the players at the tournament were that good?

He spotted Erika's reddish-brown hair in the gap between the seats in front. She was sitting on her own and had her head buried in a book.

"What are you reading?" Calum asked, squeezing his face between the seats.

Erika jerked up from her trance.

"I *was* reading *Dragonring*," she smirked, carefully folding her book around her bookmark. "Have you heard of it?"

Calum was shaking his head when, from the back of the bus, Jordan shouted, "I think we've got a hurler!"

He was teasing Lewis, whose pale skin was going green from travel sickness.

"It's your rapping that's making him ill," Sally said.

The girls' team all laughed. Calum wondered why Erika wasn't sitting with them.

"Well, you just wait for this next one," Jordan boasted, flipping his collar up.

However the track Jordan was expecting didn't come on. In fact, he didn't even need to sing. His own voice suddenly filled the bus through the speakers anyway.

Oh my loooove, don't break my hea-ah-ah-art!

"Wha— what's this?!" Jordan yelped.

"It—sounds—like—your—next—single!" Sally managed to say as she gasped for air between huge belly laughs.

Like a mob of meerkats, everyone's heads started to pop up above their seats to listen better to Jordan's home recording. Everyone apart from Lewis, who looked like he might be sick at any moment.

"I don't feel so good," he moaned.

If you leave me, ba-BY,
I would just break down and cry-ay-ay-ay

"Skip to the next track!" Jordan shouted to Mr McKlop, Coach Brown and the driver, but they were too busy talking about whatever it is that grown-ups talk about.

Lewis whined, "I'm gonnae puke."

As Mr McKlop passed back a bag for Lewis, the singing was interrupted by Jordan's mum on the recording...

"Jordi, my lamb! Your bubble bath's ready!"

"Coming Mummy!"

On hearing this, Sally and the girls fell on top of each other laughing so hard it looked like they might injure themselves.

"Oh no," Lewis whimpered, and saved Jordan from his embarrassment by throwing up into a shopping bag.

"HEUGHaaaayyyyy!"

"Yuck!"

"Mingin'!"

"Gross!"

"Look Jordan! Your singing made Lewis puke!" Sally hooted.

Mr McKlop rushed up the aisle to help Lewis, and the bus filled with the smell of sick.

Calum pulled his school jumper over his nose and looked out of the window. They had arrived in Edinburgh. There were tourists milling about taking selfies in front of a huge castle, which sat proudly on top of a massive rock.

"So that's why they're called Castle Rock Primary," Calum said quietly.

"Obvs." Leo smiled a cheeky smile and prised his eyelids apart. His afro was all dented on one side. "What'd I miss?" he yawned.

7

Caleytown and the Lion's Bottom

The bus started rumbling like thunder as it drove down a cobbled street. The buildings on either side looked like ancient skyscrapers all crammed together. Calum glanced up at a sign:

THE ROYAL MILE

"Feeling worried, Caleytown's gifted number nine?" Leo asked, punching Calum's arm.

Calum tried to laugh through his nerves.

After a brief tour of the city, the bus

finally pulled up in a car park, stopped and sighed like Calum's dad when he flopped down on the settee. All the players stretched and yawned as they stood up to get off the smelly bus.

Jordan snatched his music mix back off the startled driver, just as Lewis barrelled past him to be sick again on the tarmac.

While Coach Brown went to check on Lewis, Mr McKlop shouted, "Welcome to Holyrood Park, ladies and gentlemen." He pointed to the big, rocky hill behind him. "That's Arthur's Seat over there. It's an extinct volcano."

Calum remembered from an old lesson that Arthur's Seat was supposed to look like a resting lion. From the park he could make out the outlines of a bunch of people perched on what must be its rocky head. There was a small loch across the road. *The lion's water bowl,* Calum thought.

"Caleytown! You made it. Welcome to the annual Castle Rock Primary tournament!" A friendly woman spread her arms in front of them. Her name badge said: 'Mrs Tait'.

She busied herself with Mr McKlop and Coach Brown, getting them to sign piles and piles of forms. While the teams waited, Calum nervously scanned the crowds of players, teachers and parents.

Off to the side, there were two big white tents: one for boys to change in and one for girls. There were also a couple of portable toilets, an ice-cream van and, of course, two back-to-back pitches all set up, ready for action. The corner flags flapped in the wind.

Next to one of the flags, Calum spotted a few kids wearing Scotland Stars t-shirts. He recognised Reiss Robertson from the interview they'd watched in training. He was talking to a player who had shades on and jet-black hair fixed with gel into a side parting. He was wearing a full Hibs tracksuit. *Brandon Cramond*, Calum thought. *It had to be him.*

"Right guys, let's do this thing!" Coach Brown said as she led the girls' team to their tent. Calum, Leo and Jordan walked together with Mr McKlop. Janek, Ryan, a sickly Lewis and the rest of the squad followed them towards the boys' tent.

Out the corner of his eye, Calum thought he saw a fast-moving green shape coming towards them like a cat. *Of course it's not a cat*, he thought to himself. *There are no such things as green cats.*

When he turned back around, Brandon Cramond was standing in front of Mr McKlop, with his shades on and his hand outstretched.

"You must be Coach Iain McKlop," Brandon said, "formerly of West Lamont Primary? I'm Brandon Cramond."

Mr McKlop stared at Brandon Cramond for a while, as if to make sure he was real.

"It's *Mister* McKlop to you, Mr Cramond.
Pleased to meet you."

They shook hands slowly.

Calum and Leo stood there with their mouths hanging open. The rest of the squad looked on.

Brandon stared at Calum over his shades.

"You must be Calum Ferguson. I read that you scored a couple of good goals against Muckleton. I'm looking forward to seeing if you're as 'gifted' as Scotland Stars F.C. says you are."

Calum had never heard anyone his age speak like Brandon before. He had no idea how to respond.

"We can't wait," Leo said for him.

"Me too, Leo Nkwanu, me too," Brandon said without missing a beat. Leo was taken aback but before he could respond, Brandon Cramond was off.

"See lads, he's been preparing, just like you have," Mr McKlop said.

Calum felt like someone inside his stomach had turned the dial marked 'nerves' up to ten.

"Wow," Leo said, "if leopards could walk, talk, play football and wear bright green tracksuits, then that's what they'd be like."

First up, Burvie

"Great save, Erika!" Calum and Leo shouted from behind their friend's goal as she made another vital stop.

Caleytown's girls' team were desperately trying to hold on to a 2–1 lead against Burvie in their first match.

Mr McKlop had told the boys to show their support for the girls' team while he watched the boys from Castle Rock play Minch on the other pitch. But, when they heard a player scream out in pain, Leo and Calum couldn't help but turn their attention to the boys' match.

A tall Minch player was hobbling off with one arm around his coach and the other around a teammate. A couple of the Minch players were pointing angrily at Brandon Cramond but he was shaking his head.

"That's Minch's star player who Cramond's taken out," Leo said. "The one we read about online."

Calum shivered. If Brandon Cramond *had* been reading Scotland Stars, perhaps Leo and

'Caleytown's gifted number nine' were next.

Raised voices in the girls' game brought the boys' eyes back to Erika's match. A Burvie player was lining up a free kick within shooting range.

Calum took one look at the situation and called to Erika, "Watch out for the runner on your left."

Sure enough, the free-kick taker pretended she was going to shoot but slyly passed the ball through to her teammate instead. Thanks to Calum, Erika was ready for her!

TEAM FORMATION:

Ravi (goal keeper)

Jordan (defence)   Janek (defence)

Ryan (right wingback)   Lewis (midfield)   Leo (left wing)

Calum (striker)

Five minutes later, Calum and Leo were standing over the ball ready to kick off against Burvie. Leo's hair *still* had a dent in it from his snooze on the bus, and Lewis wasn't looking any less green after his travel sickness.

But in defence, Jordan was fired up and

ready. The fact that Brandon Cramond hadn't mentioned him by name meant he had a point to prove. Plus, he wanted to impress the girls' team after his embarrassing singing earlier. "COME ON CALEYTOWN!" he screeched so loudly that the referee dropped his whistle. Janek sighed and shook his head at his defensive partner.

The Burvie players were as big in real life as they had been in their team photo. It took their tall striker no time at all to waltz through the sleepy and queasy Caleytown team and thump a grass-cutter into the bottom corner to make it 1–0. It was an awful start but back on the halfway line, in his new boots, Calum felt strangely calm.

From the restart, Jordan screamed for a pass. Calum duly obliged and set off up the pitch.

"Pass it, Jordan!" Mr McKlop shouted from the sideline before Jordan could attempt a dribble.

Full of confidence in his new boots, Calum felt time slow down. He brought Jordan's long pass under control and jinked sideways, taking him past his marker in one movement.

Burvie's barrel-chested keeper edged forward to narrow the angle but, to Calum, the goal was the size of a house.

He bulleted a shot into the top corner to level the score. The goalie didn't even move.

"YASS!" Jordan said, running forward and punching the air. "What a pass!"

Calum shook his head and smiled down at his new boots.

Midway through the second half, a healthier-looking Lewis had a long-range shot blocked by the keeper. As it bounced back into

Calum's path, he saw the keeper was still out of position. Without breaking his stride, Calum hit a dipping volley over the sprawling keeper and into the back of the net to give Caleytown the lead at 2–1.

"What a screamer!" yelled Lewis as they celebrated the goal.

"Nice one." Leo slapped Calum's shoulder, his afro now back to its normal shape.

Calum laughed. In his new boots he felt like he could score every time he got the ball.

As the clock wound down, Calum rounded off the victory with a simple tap-in from the wingback Ryan's cross. It was his first-ever hat-trick, and it felt fantastic.

Leo ran over from the left wing with a grin on his face. "That's it, I'm buying us triple-scoop ice creams to celebrate."

Calum never said no to ice cream, but he also didn't want to stop playing. The next game couldn't come soon enough.

Brandon
Shows His Teeth

"Ice cream tastes even sweeter after a victory!"

Erika and Calum laughed as Leo held his massive three-scoop ice cream above his head like a trophy. They were watching Castle Rock's boys' team take on Burvie, the team Caleytown had just defeated.

Castle Rock had already

beaten Caleytown's next opponents, Minch, and Mr McKlop admitted that Brandon Cramond *had* injured their star player.

Calum watched Cramond prowling about the pitch. Leo's leopard comment was spot on. "Does Brandon Cramond even *have* a weakness?" Calum asked, as impressed as he was irritated by Cramond's abilities.

Erika nodded and stared off into the distance. "Talent wins games, but teamwork and intelligence win championships."

Calum and Leo just stared at her blankly.

"Michael Jordan said that," she told them.

Leo and Calum continued to stare blankly.

"*Michael Jordan*, you dorks," Erika repeated.

"One of the greatest basketball players of all time? What... nothing?" She looked from Calum to Leo for any sign that they knew who she was talking about, and sighed. "What I'm saying is Brandon's a great player but his teammates aren't all that. Plus, they're all scared of him. Watch..."

Calum watched. Erika was right. Every time a Castle Rock player got the ball they looked for Brandon straight away. They would panic and pass it to him even when it wasn't the best option. Then, whenever their passes didn't reach him, they looked like Calum's dog Leighton when he knew he'd done something bad.

"I see what you mean," Leo said, scoffing the end of his ice-cream cone. "Mind you, I'd pass to him too. He is very, very good at football."

Burvie were making things difficult for Brandon and his teammates at 0–0. In a rare attack, one of their midfielders played a one-two and ran past Brandon Cramond.

But Castle Rock's star had other ideas.

Brandon tapped his opponent's heel. It wasn't much but it was enough to send him flying through the air.

"ARGHHHH!" the Burvie player screamed as he landed. "My arm... I think... it's broken!"

Calum looked around. Surely the referee or someone else had seen Brandon's foul? But even the Burvie players weren't challenging the ref.

"Did you see that?" Calum hissed at Erika and Leo. "He tripped him on purpose!"

"I was watching the ball, Cal," Erika said. "But I don't doubt it."

Someone with 'St John's Ambulance' written on their back helped the injured player off the pitch and the game restarted. As usual, the ball found its way to Brandon Cramond like a magnet. He took no notice of his teammates and set off on a dribble from just inside his own half.

He jumped over one Burvie tackler and nutmegged another. Then, when the keeper came rushing out to dive at his feet, he calmly chipped the ball over him as if it was the easiest thing in the world to do. He didn't even bother to celebrate his goal.

On the sideline, Calum looked down at his yellow boots for comfort.

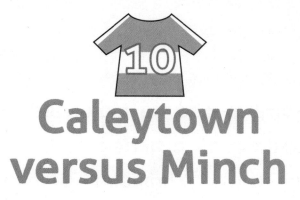

Caleytown versus Minch

In Caleytown's second match, Minch were proving to be tricky opponents.

It had started well with a quick goal from Leo. But after taking the lead so early, Caleytown relaxed too much. They soon found themselves on the wrong side of a 2–1 scoreline.

Minch kept possession so Calum's new boots couldn't make a difference. He was hardly getting a touch of the ball. The way the match

was going, Caleytown would need a slice of luck or a corner to get a goal. Midway through the second half they got both.

Calum bounced on his toes in his springy new soles and tried to ignore Brandon Cramond, who was staring at him from behind Minch's goal, with a can of juice in his hand.

"I'll run to the back post; you go to the front," Jordan whispered loudly to Calum, pushing him forward. "LEO, LEO!"

Leo surprised everyone by firing his corner low. Calum stuck a leg out and the ball pinged off his shin into the roof of the net to draw Caleytown level at 2–2.

As he ran back, Calum heard Brandon mutter,

"...not as good as he thinks he is in those stupid yellow boots."

The equaliser took the wind out of Minch's sails. Calum, Leo and Lewis could sense that the Glasgow team were low on confidence. Ever alert, Lewis intercepted a sloppy Minch pass and put Calum through on goal. The keeper dived at Calum's feet and he jumped, but not high enough.

Calum's leg clipped the keeper and he spun through the cold Edinburgh air. It felt like forever before he crashed to the ground.

"Sorry mate, ye alright?" The Minch keeper

was standing over Calum with his glove out to help him up.

The bits of his body that he'd landed on were smarting, but Calum was otherwise fine. He grabbed the keeper's glove and pulled himself up.

"I'm afraid that's a penalty," the ref said, pointing to the spot.

"Aye, nae bother, sir. It's my oan fault," Minch's keeper admitted in his strong Glaswegian accent.

Jordan had been substituted to give one of the subs a chance to play, so there was no one for Calum to argue with about taking the penalty.

He placed the ball and wiped his face with his strip. He looked up to see Brandon Cramond still standing by the goal drinking his juice. Cramond pointed at Calum's boots, said something to a teammate and laughed.

"Just look at the goal, Cal," Leo said from behind him. "Don't worry about Brandumb Cramhead."

Calum breathed out slowly and smiled to himself as he picked his spot – the top corner, right next to Brandon Cramond's face.

The referee's whistle cut through the silence.

PEEP

Calum ran up...

...struck the ball, and...

OOFt!

Brandon Cramond winced as the ball missed the goal and thumped into his stomach, sending dark juice all over his green tracksuit. "What the—" Brandon shouted. "HEY! He meant that!"

Calum was sure he could see steam rising off Brandon's red-hot, angry face. He was worried for a second that he might even storm onto the pitch.

"You'll pay for this, Calum Ferguson!" Brandon said, juice dripping off his tracksuit. Even without his shades on, his eyes looked black.

"That's quite enough drama for now," the ref said and blew his whistle. The game had finished 2–2.

Calum avoided Brandon's glare and looked up at Arthur's Seat instead. The lion stared straight ahead like he'd seen it all before.

Once the shock of hitting Brandon Cramond with the ball had worn off, Calum was gutted about missing the penalty. It would have won Caleytown the match.

"I don't know, Calum," Leo grinned cheekily, "your penalty seemed right on target to me."

"It was an... unfortunate miss, Mr Ferguson,"

Mr McKlop said, wiping his glasses, "but a win wouldn't have made a huge difference. We still need to beat Castle Rock to win the tournament." Mr McKlop got out his phone and showed them a table that was being updated minute-by-minute by the reporter Reiss Robertson.

Caleytown had won and drawn and Castle Rock had two wins. "A win is worth three points, but a draw is only worth one." Mr McKlop pointed at the screen. "Basically, if we beat Castle Rock next and get three points, we win the tournament. But if they win or we draw, the tournament is theirs."

"No bother, Mr McKlop!" said Leo, full of confidence.

ANNUAL
CASTLE ROCK PRIMARY
TOURNAMENT

LIVE FEED

TEAM	MATCHES PLAYED	POINTS	MATCHES WON	MATCHES DRAWN	MATCHES LOST
Castle Rock Primary	2	6	2	0	0
Caleytown Primary	2	4	1	1	0
Minch Primary	2	1	0	1	1
Burvie Primary	2	0	0	0	2

 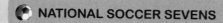

NATIONAL SOCCER SEVENS

93

Calum wasn't so sure. Facing Brandon Cramond was always going to be difficult *and* dangerous; now he had accidentally rattled the leopard's cage, who knew what Cramond would do?

The Disappearance

The thought of facing Brandon Cramond in the final match had Calum feeling nervous. So nervous, in fact, that he was desperate for the toilet.

Mr McKlop preferred that the players go in pairs at this new venue, so Lewis chummed him over to the portaloos.

"My dad is keen for me to play rugby like he did, but I like fitba," Lewis was saying. "He even put rugby posts up on our farm."

"I've never played rug—" Calum said but got distracted by a green blur at the corner of his eye. *Am I imagining things?*

"Rugby skills might come in handy if you're up against Brandon Cramond next," Lewis laughed. Calum forced a laugh too.

It least I've got my new boots, Calum thought. He did a little sprint on the spot in them to make himself feel better.

A sign on one of the two toilets said:

PLAYERZ MUST REMOVE BOOTS BEFORE ENTERING

Calum kicked his boots off. He was so desperate for the loo he couldn't see straight.

"If I go in will you look after my boots?" Calum asked Lewis.

"Sure Cal." Lewis nodded.

Calum could see clearly again when he came back out. Clearly enough to notice that there was no sign of Lewis – and no sign of his new yellow boots!

He heard some muffled whistling coming from the other cabin. *Lewis must have my boots in the other toilet,* Calum sighed with relief.

That's when he spotted Lewis's boots on the ground. *Why would he leave his and not mine?* Calum's mind raced. He heard a flush coming from Lewis' cabin. Moments later the red-haired midfielder appeared in the doorway, wiping his hands on his shorts.

Calum started to panic. "Have you got my boots?" he asked, quietly.

"Eh... no," Lewis replied looking around. "I'm still no' feeling right after that bus ride. I had to go. Sorry."

"Where are my boots then?" Calum almost shouted.

The boys looked right around the portaloos. Nothing. Lewis even gave Calum a leg up to search the roof of the toilets.

"Do I even *want* to know what's going on here?" Mr McKlop was looking up at Calum scrabbling on the toilet roof.

"Argh!" Lewis shouted as he dropped Calum and spun round to face their coach. Calum fell backwards on top of Lewis and they both tumbled to the ground. Mr McKlop just stared at them.

"I think someone's taken my boots, sir," Calum said from the ground. "I'm pretty sure I know who it was too."

"What did I say about tell-tales, Mr Ferguson?"
Mr McKlop sighed.

Calum untangled himself from Lewis and got back up. He could feel his socks getting cold and damp on the grass.

Mr McKlop's face softened when he saw the panic on Calum's face. "Ok gentlemen, I'm sure there's been a mix up. I'll ask Mrs Tait if any boots have been handed in and we'll sort everything out after our final match." He looked at his watch. "Calum, I'm sure you can borrow some boots in the meantime."

Calum slumped as he thought of Mr Aziz's son's old boots in his bag. "Yes sir."

Calum almost tripped over his bottom lip as he made his way to the changing tent in his damp socks. He found his bag and pulled out the old, taped-up boots. The leather felt dry and they creaked when he put his feet into them.

Calum tried to loosen them up by jogging on the spot but they made him feel really slow. Having worn his new boots all day, this old pair felt more uncomfortable than ever. When he saw the big crowd that had gathered for the final girls' and boys' matches, they felt even worse.

Through the gaps in the crowd, Calum could see Caleytown's girls running around the pitch. He didn't know the score but he didn't have time to find out.

"Mr Ferguson! Glad you could join us," Mr McKlop said. He had laid the water bottles out in formation.

Leo and Lewis smiled and nodded at Calum.

Jordan looked down at Calum's feet and snorted. "Why are you wearing your museum boots?"

"My new astros went *missing* when I was in the toilet," Calum replied. His face told Jordan a different story.

Jordan clearly understood Calum – he turned to search for Brandon in the crowd.

The Castle Rock captain was standing on the other side of the pitch, watching them with a crooked smile on his face.

Calum stood staring at him. He was too distracted to listen to any of Mr McKlop's pep talk until he heard his name.

"...and Calum will have to be ready to double-mark Brandon Cramond in defence with Lewis," Mr McKlop said. "It'll mean a lot more running, Calum. Are you up for it?"

Calum looked at his boots.

"Come on, Cal," Leo said, "you scored twice against Muckleton in those antiques."

Calum sighed and nodded, but he didn't think he could do anything in his old boots today.

On the pitch where the girls were still playing, the referee blew his whistle. Sally, Erika and the rest of Caleytown girls' team started shouting and screaming. By the way Coach Brown was running about with her arms in the air, it looked like Caleytown's girls had just won their tournament.

Mr McKlop started clapping. "Well done Caleytown!" He turned to his team, who were clapping too, though they were clearly all thinking about their own final. "Right lads, now it's your turn to add a trophy to the school's collection. Enjoy yourselves!"

The Winner Takes It All

The wind dropped and the clouds overhead knitted together to cut out the sun. The referee invited the two closest players, Calum and Brandon, to come forward for the coin toss.

Brandon had been glaring at Calum the whole time. The juice that Calum's shot had sprayed all over him had stained his luminous green laces a murky brown colour.

"Where did you get those boots, Ferguson?" he asked. "Did you make them yourself?"

Anger fizzed through Calum's veins but one look at Brandon's dark eyes stopped the words in his throat.

"Come on, Cal, ignore Bran Flakes, let's just enjoy this," said Leo.

Brandon ignored Leo and kept his eyes fixed on Calum. "Looks like you can't even tie your laces!"

"That's enough now, lads," the referee said cautiously before Calum or Leo could respond. Even *he* seemed a little wary of Brandon. "But your lace really is untied, number nine."

Calum looked down at his old boots, sighed, and bent down to sort them out, but the dry old lace snapped in his hand. He only just managed to make a tiny, tight knot before the ref started the match.

Still, Caleytown began pretty well. Lewis kept finding Leo in space and only some last-ditch

tackling from Castle Rock stopped Calum's best friend from scoring.

Keeping to Mr McKlop's strategy, Calum was doing his best to double up with Lewis against Brandon whenever Castle Rock had possession. It was hard work in his old boots, and if the pain in his feet wasn't enough, Brandon kept jabbing at Calum's ribs with his elbow, standing on his toes or pinching him whenever he got the chance.

After some hard running back and forth, Calum finally had the ball at his feet – but not for long. Brandon barged him off the ball and slunk up the pitch like a cat with its prey.

A pumped-up Jordan charged out to tackle

but Brandon weaved past him as if he was just some minor nuisance.

Ravi's quiff wobbled as he spread himself wide in goals...

THWOP!

Brandon bulleted the ball into the bottom corner. The big crowd cheered and this time Castle Rock's star did celebrate. He made sure to run right past Calum on his way back to his half.

Feeling hopeless, Calum buried his face in his strip.

"Cheer up," an unfamiliar voice murmured. "At least you don't have to play with him every week."

Calum pulled his shirt back down so he

could see who had spoken. A Castle Rock player shrugged and gave him a weak smile.

Even his teammates hate him, thought Calum.

Leo slapped Calum on the shoulder. "Don't give up yet, Cal! We can still win this!"

As if to prove his point Leo ran straight forward from the restart. Calum ran as fast as his old boots would let him, just to keep up. Leo drifted out wide before squaring the ball back to Lewis, who picked out Calum in the box with a first-time pass.

The crowd held its breath.

Calum took an extra touch in his old boots to control the ball, drew his leg back to shoot and...

BANG!

A bump on his shoulder sent him spinning to the ground.

"Penalty, ref!" Calum heard Lewis shout as he pushed himself up onto all fours.

The referee blew his whistle.

Yes! Calum thought. *I'll show you, Brandon!*

"That's half-time, lads," the referee said.

Calum shook his head in disbelief, got up and made his way over to Mr McKlop. He looked over his shoulder and caught Brandon's eye. He was laughing.

"Did you see that foul, Mr McKlop?" Calum complained to his coach. "He totally took me out! That should have been a penalty!"

"Now, now, Calum. You've got to respect the ref's decision – even if you disagree with it," said Mr McKlop with a frown.

Calum angrily shook his head. "It's not right though. The ref's scared of a nine year old!"

Mr McKlop scratched his chin. "Hey, Calum, why don't you take some time out."

The fire that was burning in Calum's stomach went out as Mr McKlop handed him a bib.

13

How to Beat a Player Like Brandon Cramond

Calum sat on the sideline pulling blades of grass out of the ground while his teammates tried to get an equaliser.

During a pause in the action, Brandon gave Calum a sarcastic wave. Calum felt sick.

"Whatcha doin' Cal?" Erika appeared over him. "Digging for treasure?"

Calum didn't say anything.

Erika sat down next to him. She'd changed out of her strip and already had her bag packed.

"Aren't you going to say congratulations?" she asked.

"What? Oh... sorry, congratulations! You were great." Calum tried to smile.

"I thought we might win too, but..." Calum

pointed at Brandon just as Lewis tried to wrestle the ball off him.

"WAY TO GO, LEWIS!" Erika shouted towards the pitch, then turned back to Calum. "Did you let Brandon the Bully get the better of you?"

"Well, no, but, yes, but... I lost my new astros!" Calum whined.

"So what?" said Erika, to Calum's surprise. "You were man of the match against Muckleton before you had fancy new astros. Boots don't matter Cal, not really."

Calum didn't want to argue with Erika. He stared out at the pitch instead, where he saw Lewis play a lovely, curling pass round Brandon to Leo on the wing. Brandon's fists were clenched at his sides.

"It's easy, Cal," Erika said, pulling her book out of her bag. "Like the dragon-fighting guy in my book, you've just gotta find your enemy's weakness."

"That's the point: Brandon doesn't have one," Calum moaned.

"Umm... yeah he does," Erika said. "My mom always says 'pride comes before a fall'."

Calum looked blank.

"Well, dummy, Brandon is too proud. His game is all about being the best. All you gotta do is show him you're better," Erika said, getting excited. "And you *are* better Cal. I've overheard loads of people around here talking about your amazing hat-trick in the first match."

"Really?" Calum asked. He hadn't read Erika's book about dragons but he could feel fire beginning to burn in his belly again.

"Really." Erika nodded.

On the pitch Janek played the ball to Lewis. Lewis looked for Leo again but before he could send the ball anywhere, Brandon's knee found Lewis's thigh.

"ARGH!" Lewis shouted as he fell to the ground. "Ref! He did that on purpose!"

"It was an accident," the referee said, looking

down at Lewis. "We'll restart with a dropped ball."

"Sorry," Brandon said flatly. He held his hand out to help Lewis up. Lewis tried to get up himself but his dead leg was too sore. Mr McKlop jogged onto the pitch to help.

Their coach walked Lewis back to where Calum was sitting at the sidelines and put his hand on Calum's shoulder. "You're back on. Same role as before." Mr McKlop paused thoughtfully. "You do know why Brandon fouled you, don't you?"

Calum shook his head.

"He's scared you'll show him up. He knows you're a better player than him."

The fire in Calum's belly was burning like a furnace now.

"I want you to go out there and show the rest of this crowd what he's scared of," said Mr McKlop.

Lewis gave a half-grin, half-wince in agreement, clutching his leg. "Come on, Cal, show him how we play football in Caleytown!"

"You go Cal!" shouted Erika in agreement, clapping him as he ran on.

Calum's boots creaked and groaned but he wasn't listening to them any more. He sprinted over to stand nose-to-nose with Brandon, ready for the restart.

Penalty!

"Was that your *girlfriend* sitting next to you on the sidelines?" Brandon asked. Calum ignored him. It was surprisingly easy to do so.

The ref dropped the ball.

Calum was first to react and thumped it to Leo. He sprung forward and barrelled past Brandon, pointing to where he wanted Leo to put the ball. Leo smiled and chipped a lovely pass in behind Castle Rock's defence.

Calum, with Brandon in pursuit, flew past

Castle Rock's last defender like a racing car past a grandstand. But as he got ready to shoot he felt Brandon's studs rake right down the back of his leg, trap his boot-heel and pull his old boot clean off.

Not this time, Calum thought. He kept his balance and smashed the ball past the Castle Rock keeper with nothing but a sock on his foot.

A huge cheer went up around the pitch.

You go Cal!

What a strike!

Calum didn't celebrate his equaliser, or rub his stinging foot. Instead, he picked up his boot and strolled past Brandon, who just stood, staring at the ball in the back of the net. 1–1.

Castle Rock could win the tournament with a draw in this match, and they made sure they kept possession in Caleytown's half to wind the clock down. Leo hopped up and down on his toes in frustration.

"Be ready!" Leo shouted to Calum over his shoulder.

Calum didn't even have time to shout back "For what?" before his friend disappeared into a group of blue strips.

Moments later, he reappeared with the ball like a high-speed train out of a tunnel.

Calum's feet started moving before his brain had time to figure out what was happening. On the wing, Leo jinked past a challenge and took off up the pitch.

Brandon Cramond arrived right on cue to keep Calum company, but Caleytown's gifted number nine was full of confidence. Calum dummied Leo's pass and let the ball roll through his – and Brandon's – legs. He spun round his confused opponent and met the ball on the other side.

The crowd cheered.

Calum was in full flow now. To beat the last

defender, he scissored his left leg over the ball but went right. This was it. This was the big chance.

Calum drew his leg back to shoot and...

OOFt!

He felt a knee smash into the back of his left leg.

Calum collapsed to the ground. He could hear the crowd jeering. Brandon was standing over him and smirking.

Take Two

The referee blew his whistle.

PEEEEEP!

Oh no, it can't be full-time already? Calum thought, holding his leg where it hurt. Caleytown still needed another goal to win the game, and the tournament.

Suddenly some of the crowd's jeers turned

to cheers, and vice versa. Calum looked up to see the referee pointing to the spot! It was a penalty to Caleytown!

"No way referee!" Brandon shouted. "Look! His lace is untied again. He clearly tripped himself up!"

"That's enough Mr Cramond," the referee said. "You know exactly what happened. You weren't even *trying* to get the ball that time."

Jordan came sprinting forward and grabbed the ball for the penalty but then stopped. He looked down at Calum on the ground trying to tie the lace on his old boot. Then he took a good look at Brandon Cramond.

"Go on then, Museum Boots," Jordan said, pulling Calum to his feet. "You'd better score this time though."

"This is the last kick of the match, lads," said the referee.

Calum felt a hundred pairs of eyes watching him as he placed the ball on the penalty spot. This time it was Erika, not Brandon, standing behind the goals. She smiled and nodded.

Calum took three steps back and heard Brandon say, "Careful not to hit your *girlfriend*."

"Shut it," said Jordan, of all people. The referee shot him a look.

Calum breathed out slowly, picked his spot and started his run up.

Step
step,
step...
THWACK!

The crowd held its breath as the ball swung towards goal. The keeper had chosen the right way and stretched his arm out. The ball brushed his finger tips and...

CLUNK!

Calum's shot hit the underside of the crossbar and...

SWOOSH!

flew into the back of the net!

The referee blew his whistle for full-time. 2–1! Caleytown had won! Calum disappeared under a pile of yellow Caleytown players.

Calum looked around for Brandon. He had already vanished into the crowd.

The Ceremony

"I like the way this feels around my neck," Leo said, admiring his gold medal. Calum nodded.

"Me too," Erika agreed, polishing hers with a sleeve.

Behind them, Mr McKlop was speaking to Coach Brown. "I think we might be ready to enter a bigger competition, you know."

"Awesome, Iain. Let's do it!" said Coach Brown with her usual enthusiasm. "We've got great teams on our hands here."

Calum and Leo smiled at each other and bumped fists. But Calum's excitement was being ruined by the dread of having to tell his parents about his yellow boots. Mr McKlop had done everything he could to help find them. It was no good; they had vanished.

Mrs Tait started another speech. "The coaches have picked their players of the tournament."

Calum and Leo looked at each other.

"Please step forward... Erika Brown and Calum Ferguson!"

Mrs Tait started clapping and the rest of the crowd quickly joined in. Calum stood frozen to the spot.

Leo pushed him forwards. "Go on Cal!"

Calum walked past Brandon in the crowd. He was picking mud out of his boots to avoid clapping.

Calum didn't see Brandon again until he was on his way back to the bus. Castle Rock's captain was standing next to an expensive car waiting for his dad to get off his phone. They were both wearing sunglasses.

Brandon nodded as Calum passed him. "Congratulations, Calum Ferguson."

"Thanks," Calum said, a little confused by Brandon's politeness. He'd had more than enough of him for one day and just wanted to get on the bus.

"Maybe we'll play again some time in the future?" Brandon said. He had his tracksuit top tied around his waist but you could still see juice stains on his trousers.

"Maybe," Calum said. He had to bite his lip to stop himself from accusing Brandon of stealing his boots. Judging by his dad's fancy car, he didn't need to nick other people's kit.

Brandon stared at Calum's feet. "Listen," he said. "I—"

"Stop chatting to your wee friend and get in the car, Brandon, we're already late," Brandon's dad barked.

Brandon turned his back on Calum and slid into the passenger seat. His dad revved the engine and they spun away.

"What was all that about?" Leo asked, appearing at Calum's shoulder.

"No idea." Calum shrugged.

Bus and Boots

At the team bus, Coach Brown was counting the Caleytown players back on. Calum tapped Jordan on the shoulder.

"Hey Jordan, thanks for letting me take the penalty."

"Whatever. Just as well you scored," Jordan said, before turning round to Lewis who was limping up the stairs. "You'd better not barf on me, Hop-along!"

"Don't worry *Jordi*," Sally sang from behind

Calum. "You can always wash it off in your bubble bath tonight!"

The girls' team all burst out laughing. Coach Brown turned away but you could see her shoulders shaking with giggles. Jordan could have heated the water for his bubble bath with his bright red face.

Back in their seats, Leo grinned. "That. Was. Ace. Sorry about your boots though."

"Yeah, I know," Calum sighed. "My dad's going to go mental. I'm so sure—"

The bus driver woke the engine up and Leo started yawning right away.

"Unbelievable," Calum laughed. Leo just winked. Calum leaned forwards towards Erika's seat, squeezing his face between the gap. "Hey Erika, could I borrow that book you were talking about? Sleeping Beauty is already drifting off." He pointed at Leo, who was mid-yawn again.

Calum didn't hear Erika's answer. He was distracted by the noise of what sounded like a dog running along the bus's roof as the driver rolled out of the car park. He followed the noise with his eyes as it made its way along the roof until... two flashes of yellow dropped past the bus's window!

"MY BOOTS!" Calum shouted. "STOP THE BUS!"

Mr McKlop had heard the noise too and was already asking the driver to stop. Calum bounded down the aisle.

"You won't need your trophy to fetch them, Calum," Mr McKlop said, smiling. Calum looked at his hand and laughed. He was still clutching his player-of-the-tournament award. Mr McKlop offered to hold it.

Curious eyes watched Calum from the bus as he ran around it. Sure enough, there on the ground lay his brand new yellow astros. The laces had been tied together. Someone must have lobbed them on the bus's roof.

At that moment, Calum didn't care if Brandon had done it or not, he was just relieved to have his boots back.

"Maybe leopards like to play with yellow astros, Mr Ferguson?" Mr McKlop said from behind Calum. "Come on, let's take our trophies back to Caleytown."

Calum smiled and followed his teacher to the bus door. He took one last look at Arthur's Seat. He knew he would never forget playing in his first proper tournament, under the gaze of the ancient lion's rocky eyes.

DANNY SCOTT, a die-hard football fan, works for Scottish Book Trust and is the goalie for Scotland Writers F.C.

ALICE A. MORENTORN is a children's book illustrator and a teacher at Emile Cohl School of Arts in Lyon, France.

ANNUAL CASTLE ROCK PRIMARY TOURNAMENT

CALEYTOWN BOYS BREAK THROUGH CASTLE ROCK IN CUP SHOCK
REISS ROBERTSON REPORTS

Caleytown spoiled Castle Rock's annual party in Holyrood Park, Edinburgh, this weekend. The unfancied side from Scotland's central belt trumped 'The Rocks' with a last-minute penalty conceded by their surly star Brandon Cramond.

The scorer, Calum Ferguson, seemed to be wearing boots held together by tape in the final game. However, it didn't affect his ability to dispatch the winning spot kick past Castle Rock's keeper.

Ferguson took home a player-of-the-tournament award for his outstanding performances, including a memorable hat-trick against Burvie Primary in Caleytown's opening match.

The boys' success was matched only by the Caleytown girls' team and their prodigal goalie Erika Brown. Perhaps this was a one-off for Caleytown. Or, perhaps it's the start of a special season for the yellow-and-whites under the expert guidance of Mr Iain McKlop and coach Shannon Brown. Stay tuned to Scotland Stars F.C. to find out.

Email: fitba@scotlandstarsfc.co.uk for your thoughts on the action.

RUMOURS & GOSSIP

⚽ Caleytown's girls' team took home the silverware aided by player-of-the-tournament performances from their American-born goalkeeper Erika Brown.

⚽ Our special haircut of the tournament goes to Caleytown's keeper Ravi. His quiff was the stand-up performer of the day.

⚽ Scotland Stars' national tournament kicks off next month. Make sure your team's involved to be in with a chance of qualifying for our annual national showdown at the Heroes Glen indoor arena next March.

⚽ Scotland Stars would love to know about the best goal you've ever scored. Describe it to fitba@scotlandstarsfc.co.uk

TOURNAMENT RESULTS

TEAM	MATCHES PLAYED	POINTS	MATCHES WON	MATCHES DRAWN	MATCHES LOST
Caleytown Primary	3	7	2	1	0
Castle Rock Primary	3	6	2	0	1
Minch Primary	3	2	0	2	1
Burvie Primary	3	2	0	1	2

 Par Excellence!

This game is just like golf! Place a marker – a jacket or cone will do – and set a starting point quite far away. Now, just like golf, see how many passes it takes before you or your friend hit the marker with the ball.
The lowest score wins.

For an extra challenge, try using alternate feet. Or focus on using your weaker foot, if you have one.

DESIGN YOUR OWN STRIP!

GRAB THE WHISTLE

1. A player has a clean shot on goal when their teammate, who is on a hat trick, barges them off the ball and scores. What do you do?

a) Award the goal
b) Show them both a yellow card
c) Scratch your head

If you were the referee, would you make the right call?

2. What is the minimum number of players a team can have on the pitch in an eleven-a-side match?

a) Nine
b) Seven
c) One: the goalie

3. A player takes a throw-in that never makes it onto the pitch. How do you react?

a) With belly laughs
b) Order them to retake the throw-in
c) Give the throw-in to the other team

Answers: 1a, 2b, 3b